ALSO BY JOE LASKER

Tales of a Seadog Family

Merry Ever After:
THE STORY OF
TWO MEDIEVAL WEDDINGS

TRANGE VOYAGE OF
NEPTUNE'S CAR

written and illustrated by JOE LASKER

The Viking Press
New York

FOR HELEN AND NATHAN

First Edition
Copyright © Joe Lasker, 1977
All rights reserved
First published in 1977 by The Viking Press
625 Madison Avenue, New York, N.Y. 10022
Published simultaneously in Canada by
Penguin Books Canada Limited
Printed in U.S.A.

1   2   3   4   5   81   80   79   78   77

Library of Congress Cataloging in Publication Data
Lasker, Joe.   The strange voyage of Neptune's Car.
Summary: Young Mary Anne Patten becomes the first
woman to command a clipper ship when her husband, the
ship's captain, falls ill during the hazardous voyage
around Cape Horn and she is the only one aboard capable
of navigating.
1. Patten, Mary Anne (Brown), 1837– 1861 —Juvenile
fiction. 2. Patten, Joshua A., 1826 or 1827– 1857—Juvenile
fiction. 3. Neptune's Car (Clipper ship)—Juvenile
fiction. [1. Patten, Mary Anne (Brown), 1837– 1861 —Fiction.
2. Patten, Joshua A., 1826 or 1827– 1857—Fiction.
3. Neptune's Car (Clipper ship)—Fiction] I. Title.
PZ7.L3272St   [Fic.]   77-22749
ISBN 0-670-67742-6

The author gratefully acknowledges the assistance of Commander Everett H. Northrop, U. S. M. S., Librarian, U. S. Merchant Marine Academy, Kings Point, New York; Mr. George D. Wintress, Vice President, The Seamen's Bank for Savings, New York; Pamela McNulty, Reference Librarian, Mystic Seaport, Connecticut; and Anita Wilcox and Richard Seidman, Norwalk, Connecticut.

*A*ROUND THE WORLD AGAIN! On July 1, 1856, Joshua and Mary Patten set sail from New York on their second voyage.

As they sailed out of the harbor, Mary thought of the beginning of their first voyage almost two years before. She blushed as she remembered what a homesick, seasick landlubber she had been. How she had missed her mother and her home!

On that first voyage she had been bored and lonely. To fill time she had decided to learn all about the ship.

Joshua taught her navigation: how to find where the ship was in the vast ocean, how to figure the direction it should sail, and how to find the distance it had sailed from one point to another. The voyage lasted a year and a half, and when it was over Mary was in love with ships and the sea.

Joshua Patten was Mary's husband. The great clipper ship, NEPTUNE'S CAR, was his first command. Only captains could take their families along on a sea voyage — that is how Mary came to be sailing.

The sailors called Joshua "The Old Man," and Mary "The Old Woman," even though Joshua was only twenty-nine and Mary nineteen.

"We are in a race, Mary," Joshua said that day. "Two other clippers left New York the same time as NEPTUNE'S CAR, all steering the same course. It's 15,000 miles to San Francisco, and I hope we can win." Just then the lookout shouted, "Sail ho!" One of the other clippers had been sighted.

After several weeks at sea, the weather changed. Cold winds blew and a heavy snow fell. Joshua shook his head. "If the weather is so bad up here, what is it like down there at Cape Horn?"

NEPTUNE'S CAR *spoke to the* RAPID, *limping north to Rio for repairs and a new crew.*

Her captain told Joshua, "We tried to fight our way around Cape Horn. After forty days the first mate and nine seamen were lost overboard. The rest of us are sick or crippled. I had to turn back. It's the worst Cape winter in memory. If I were you, I'd turn back now."

The harsh weather made for hard work and mean tempers. Mr. Keeler, the first mate and a cruel man, beat and cursed the crew even more than usual.

Mr. Hare, the second mate, the opposite of Mr. Keeler, was cheerful and helpful, even in bad weather, but he too worried about what lay ahead.

Mary could see that Mr. Keeler disliked her and the captain. She felt troubled. One night when Mr. Keeler was on watch, he fell asleep. The ship was endangered. A wind shift caused the sails to go loose and flap wildly, making a loud noise and changing the ship's direction. The noise, like the snapping of a whip, awoke Joshua and Mary.

Joshua dashed up on deck, and when he saw Keeler asleep he was furious. The wind could have torn the sails. He kicked Keeler awake and ordered, "Call the crew to trim the sails, then report to me in the cabin!"

Waiting in the dining saloon, Mary could hear Joshua's angry voice. "Mr. Keeler, you endangered the ship and everyone on board! You set a terrible example for the crew just when we are nearing Cape Horn. I warn you, abandon your duty once more and you will be kept under arrest all the way to San Francisco!" The first mate did not reply.

Awful! Awful! Joshua discovered Keeler sleeping on watch again and ordered him locked in his cabin, under arrest. Now Joshua had to add Mr. Keeler's duties to his own.

Ahead lay Cape Horn.

Howling winds and knife-edged sleet hit the ship, coating it in

ice. Joshua was topside day and night, doing his own and the first mate's work, while Mary stayed below.

The captain caught what sleep he could, sitting in a chair lashed to the rail to keep from being washed overboard. Mary worried about him because he was always cold and wet. Even his food was icy and soaked by the time the steward could get it to him.

During a lull in the storm, Joshua joined Mary in the cabin. He was coughing and shivering with fever. She begged him to rest and to put Mr. Hare, the second mate, in charge until he felt better. Joshua refused.

Then Mary told him, "Joshua, before NEPTUNE'S CAR returns to New York, you will be a father. I can't rest easy with you so sick, staying up on deck day and night. Please, get some rest."

Joshua touched her hand gently and said, "How wonderful that we are going to have a baby! You will need your rest." He sighed, "Get Mr. Hare."

When Joshua explained to the second mate why he was being given command of the ship, Mr. Hare answered, "Sir, I can handle the ship and the men all right. The problem is I don't know how to read or write or reckon." He pointed to the navigating instruments, maps, and logbooks on the table. Joshua looked at Mary, and they felt each other's helplessness and fear.

Driven by roaring winds, NEPTUNE'S CAR *reached Cape Horn. Moun-tainous waves thundered over the rail. Joshua, still sick, was up on deck. Mary asked Mr. Hare to stay near Joshua...just in case.*

At noon Mr. Hare burst into Mary's cabin carrying Joshua, who was unconscious. Mr. Hare had grabbed him just in time to save him from being swept overboard by a wave.

As they put Joshua to bed, Mr. Hare said, "You will have to take over, ma'am!"

"What do you mean?"

"It's you or Keeler," answered Mr. Hare. "You two are the only ones left who can navigate, and nobody trusts Keeler."

"But I must stay by the captain's side now and look after him."

"You must take command!" Mr. Hare said. "The ship must be saved first! Make the captain comfortable. I'll see to the ship and crew and then report back to you for orders." Mary knew he was right—she must save the ship.

For the next two nights she did not sleep. She nursed Joshua and plotted the ship's course by "dead reckoning" through heavy fog, avoiding the rocky coast. Icebergs, like phantoms, loomed up unexpectedly. Somehow the ship kept going. Mr. Hare cheerfully followed Mary's commands.

The ship groaned and shuddered from the pounding of the seas. Joshua shivered with fever. He could not see or hear. Mary studied the ship's medical books to learn how to treat his illness and learned that Joshua had "brain fever." "I feel so alone, so tired," she said to herself, and began to weep. "Oh, Mama, how I wish you were here to comfort me!"

The next day Mary and Mr. Hare were on deck. She shouted to be heard over the roar of the sea and wind. "The crew is so brave! Look

how they risk death, climbing up the slippery, icy rigging in this blinding wind. Their fingers are bleeding, cracked and numbed from the cold!" Mary and Mr. Hare watched as the sailors untied frozen knots and clawed at the ice-coated sails that weighed tons.

From that night on Mary decided she would sleep in her clothing to be ready for any emergency.

Before daybreak, Mary was suddenly awakened and called up on deck. Three seamen, aloft on the wildly swaying topsail yard, had just been blown off into the sea. "Lost! Lost!" Mary cried out. Already half the crew was helplessly sick. The ship will be crippled if we lose more men, she thought. What will I do then?

Again Mary got no sleep. There was too much to do. Waves, like walls of water, boarded the ship. NEPTUNE'S CAR was soaked. The cook's fires were drenched: there was no hot food, no way to dry out their wet clothing.

Mr. Keeler sent Mary a note begging to be returned to duty and promising he would bring the ship safely to San Francisco. Mary tore it up angrily. "Does he think I can forget how he put us all in danger?" she said. "He thinks I'm a fool because I'm a woman. But I know if he was ever in command he would take revenge on Joshua, who is sick and helpless. Let him stay where he is."

"We did it!" shouted Mr. Hare, bursting into the cabin and awakening Mary. She had fallen asleep sitting at Joshua's bedside. "Cape Horn couldn't stop us. We have just sailed into the Pacific Ocean."

Mary leaped to her feet. She looked at Joshua, who was still unconscious. How she wished she could tell him! Then she turned to Mr. Hare and said, "We brought this gallant clipper around the Horn in eighteen days. I'm proud of the crew." They shook hands. The weather cleared briefly as if to celebrate, and sunlight danced on the water. How good to be alive, Mary thought to herself.

But there was still Mr. Keeler. He tried to stir up the crew to mutiny against Mary. He sent them messages: "Are you mad, letting a nineteen-year-old girl sail this clipper? She is bad luck! Three men died off Cape Horn. The captain is dying. Don't let her turn this ship into a coffin. Get rid of her!"

Mr. Hare advised Mary. "Trust the men. They don't want Keeler to be their captain. They remember how he beat them and cursed them. They remember he endangered the ship by sleeping when he was on watch." Mary thought this advice was good, and she paid no further attention to Mr. Keeler.

Trade winds and the warm southern sun favored NEPTUNE'S CAR. *She raced along almost on her own, allowing Mary more time to nurse Joshua. Sometimes his sight and hearing returned to him for a while.*

Working over her charts and maps one day, Mary saw that the ship was nearing California. Soon the strange voyage of NEPTUNE'S CAR *will be over, Mary thought. I'll miss this ship. I'm proud to be its commander and proud that I navigated safely for 8000 miles.*

One morning NEPTUNE'S CAR *sailed into San Francisco Bay as crowds along the docks watched her come in. Mary could see the other captains studying her closely through long telescopes. She smiled. Their puzzled faces showed surprise that a woman was at the captain's post.*

Before noon the sails came down and the clipper was snugged in at the dock.

Joshua was rushed to the hospital. Two armed guards took Mr. Keeler to the city jail. Close friends met the ship and brought Mary to their home.

"What a brave thing you did, Mary," they said to her. Mary looked across the bay to the open sea.

"For the past fifty nights I have slept in my clothing. Tonight I hope to have a hot bath, and sleep in my comfortable nightgown, in a soft, dry bed. I hope Joshua will be all right." Then she sighed, "I'm so tired."

*I*N THE RACE with the two other clippers, *Neptune's Car* finished second, reaching San Francisco on November 15, 1856, after a trip of four and a half months. Mary Patten is the only woman who ever commanded a clipper, and one of the very few women in history to command any large seagoing ship.

Captain Joshua Patten, blind and deaf, died in Massachusetts on July 25, 1857, four months after the birth of his son, Joshua Jr.

Mary Patten died on March 17, 1861, of an illness brought on by the rigors of the voyage.

The Hospital at the United States Merchant Marine Academy, King's Point, New York, is named in memory of Mary Patten.

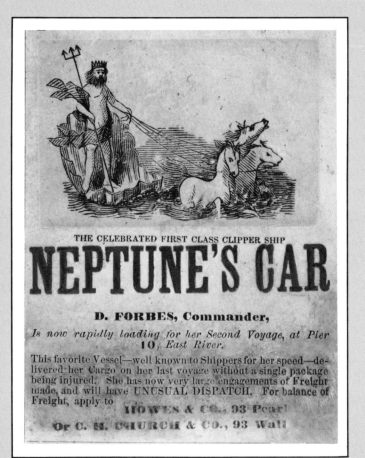

THE CELEBRATED FIRST CLASS CLIPPER SHIP

NEPTUNE'S CAR

D. FORBES, Commander,

Is now rapidly loading for her Second Voyage, at Pier 10, East River.

This favorite Vessel—well known to Shippers for her speed—delivered her Cargo on her last voyage without a single package being injured. She has now very large engagements of Freight made, and will have UNUSUAL DISPATCH. For balance of Freight, apply to

HOWES & CO., 93 Pearl

Or C. H. CHURCH & CO., 93 Wall

The Celebrated and Favorite Extreme
Clipper Ship

NEPTUNE'S CAR

DANIEL H. BEARSE, Commander,

Is now receiving Cargo at PIER 15 E. R., foot of Wall St.

This ship is now rendered famous for having performed her last voyage under the most trying circumstances; when, during the severe illness of her able commander, Capt. PATTEN, she was successfully commanded and navigated for 54 days by his heroic wife, who, without the assistance of any officers, succeeded in taking the ship safely into the port of San Francisco; and yet, under all these circumstances, making a quick passage. It is only necessary further to refer shippers to the fact that this fine vessel has made the voyage to San Francisco in 105 and 97 days. She insures at lowest rates. Dispatch as above may be relied upon. For Freight, apply to

WM. T. COLEMAN & CO., 88 Wall St.,

TONTINE BUILDING.

Agents at San Francisco, Messrs. WM. T. COLEMAN & CO.

New York—San Francisco